This book belongs to:

_____

_____

_____

First published by Walker Books Ltd.
87 Vauxhall Walk, London SE11 5HJ

Copyright © 2003 by Lucy Cousins
Lucy Cousins font copyright © 2003 by Lucy Cousins
Illustrated in the style of Lucy Cousins by King Rollo Films Ltd.

"Maisy" audio visual series produced by King Rollo Films Ltd.
for Universal Pictures International Visual Programming

Maisy™. Maisy is a registered trademark of Walker Books Ltd., London.

First U.S. edition 2003

Library of Congress Cataloging-in-Publication Data is available.
Library of Congress Catalog Card Number 2003040939

ISBN 0-7636-2196-X

Printed in China

This book was typeset in Lucy Cousins.
The illustrations were done in gouache.

Candlewick Press
2067 Massachusetts Avenue
Cambridge, Massachusetts 02140

visit us at www.candlewick.com

Maisy's Snowy Christmas Eve

Lucy Cousins

CANDLEWICK PRESS
CAMBRIDGE, MASSACHUSETTS

It was
Christmas Eve.

Snow fell on
Maisy's house.

Snow fell on
Charley's
house.

Snow fell on
Cyril's house.

Snow fell on
Tallulah's
house.

Snow fell on Eddie!

He was on his way
to see Maisy.

Everyone was invited to Maisy's house for Christmas.

Cyril went on snowshoes and got there slowly.

Charley and Tallulah
went by sled
and got there
quickly.

Eddie went
by foot ...
and got stuck
in the snow!

At Maisy's house the snow
fell thick and fast.

And it was COLD!

The friends hurried inside
to get warm by the fire.

Tallulah and Cyril
hung stockings.

But where was Eddie?

Maisy and Charley made
mince pies and
paper chains.

But where was Eddie?

Everyone helped
decorate
the tree.

But where was Eddie?

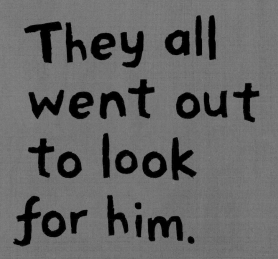

They all
went out
to look
for him.

They found a shed covered in snow.

They found a bush covered in snow.

They found snow covered in snow...

and finally they found
Eddie covered
in snow.

But poor Eddie was stuck!

Then Maisy had an idea.
She got the tractor.

One, two, three...

At last, Eddie was free.

That night,
everyone gathered
around the tree to
sing Christmas carols.